THE CHUPACABRA ATE THE CANDELABRA

Marc Tyler Nobleman • illustrated by Ana Aranda

NANCY PAULSEN BOOKS

As the sun set, the goats met.

"Tonight could be the night," Jayna said. "The night the chupacabra comes for dinner."

"On such short notice? But we have nothing prepared!" Bumsie said. "By the way, what's a chupacabra?"

"Let's put it this way. He would not *join* us for dinner. He would *eat* us for dinner."

"How impolite," Pep said.

W-what does the Chupacabra eat for
b-breakfast?" Bumsie said.

"Goats," Jayna said.

"F-for l-lunch?"

"More goats."

"No veggies?" Pep said, shaking his head.

"Not healthy."

"I know how we can save ourselves!" Bumsie said.
"Wait ∼ can the chupacabra climb trees?"
"I hear he can," Jayna said. "Besides, you can't."
"Right," Bumsie said. "So I'll just stick with being frightened."

"Come on, goats!" Jayna said. "I say we find the chupacabra before he finds us! I say we scare him off before he eats us! Who's with me?" Nobody answered.

"I said, who's with me?"

"Silly," Bumsie said. "Everyone is right here."

"I mean who's *going* with me."

"I would . . . ," Pep said, "but it's too dark."

"Not with this," Jayna said,
whipping out a candelabra.

"Line up!" Jayna said. "Bravest in back, most frightened in front."

"Don't you mean 'most frightened in back'?" Bumsie said.

"No," Jayna said. "If the most frightened is in back, he'll have no one to watch behind him."

"Line up! Bravest in back, me and the candelabra in front," Bumsie said.

The goats filed nervously across the plains.

"Just how are we going to scare the chupacabra?" Pep said.

"There's lots of us and only one of him," Jayna said. "That's all I've thought of so far."

Soon Bumsie felt something other than grass underfoot.

"*Welcome*? Ha! That mat won't fool us," Jayna said. "It's a trap."

"The trap is delicious," Bumsie said.

"You know what else is delicious?" a voice said from the darkness.

The chupacabra jumped out.
"Eek!" the goats called out.
Poof! The lights went out.
The candelabra was gone.

"THE CHUPACABRA ATE THE CANDELABRA!"

"He swallowed it whole!"
Pep said. "But I thought the
only thing he eats is ~"

"Goats!" the chupacabra said. "Candelabras are my
third-favorite thing! Did you bring more? I'm still hungry.
I'm always hungry."

"Sorry, we didn't," Jayna said.

"Then whatever shall I eat next?" the chupacabra said.

"I recommend veggies," Pep said. "And chewing."

"Or . . . ," Bumsie said, "we can get you another candelabra."

"Oh, would it be any trouble?"

"Not at all. We'll be back," Bumsie said. "With me *in* back."

The goats headed home to worry.
"That was the only candelabra I had,"
Jayna said.

"But if we feed him more, maybe he won't eat *us*," Bumsie said.

"We have to find another candelabra," Pep said, "or else ～"

"Nice place you have here," the chupacabra said,
stepping out of the sunlight.

"¡Ay, caramba!" the goats shrieked.

"I came by just to tell you that I'm more in the mood
for my *second*-favorite thing to eat."

"Might you mean weeds?" Jayna said. "If so, it's our ∼
I mean your ∼ lucky day!"

"No," the chupacabra said. "What I crave are . . . cucarachas. And what do you know ~ here comes one now!"

The chupacabra snatched it up and gulped it down.

"THE CHUPACABRA ATE THE CUCARACHA!"

"Might you have any more?" the chupacabra said.

"We don't, I'm afraid," Jayna said.

"I'm also afraid," Bumsie said, scampering off.

"No cucarachas? No candelabras?" the chupacabra said.

"We're sorry again," Jayna said.

"No problem," the chupacabra said. "Because you *do* have my *favorite* thing to eat."

Jayna and Pep shuddered.

"Please let *that* be weeds," Pep said.

"Would I come all this way for weeds? No, my favorite thing to eat is . . ."

"A CANDELABRA!"

Bumsie said, scampering back. "Thank goat I found one!"

"But that's my *third*-favorite thing to eat, remember?"

"A CUCARACHA!"

Pep said, spotting one on the ground. "Just in time!"

"But that's my ∽ "

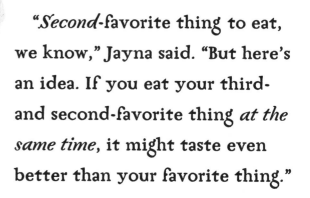

"*Second*-favorite thing to eat, we know," Jayna said. "But here's an idea. If you eat your third- and second-favorite thing *at the same time*, it might taste even better than your favorite thing."

The chupacabra tried it.

"THE CHUPACABRA ATE THE CANDELABRA AND THE CUCARACHA!"

"Thank you for the suggestion," the chupacabra said, "but that was gross."

The chupacabra straightened up and smacked his lips.
"As I was saying, my *favorite* thing to eat is . . .

The goats sighed with relief.

"There's lots of us and only one of you," Jayna said. "You'll have so much goat cheese, you'll never be hungry."

"But I'm *always* hungry," the chupacabra said. "So I'll eat *anything*."

Bumsie's relief was brief. "D-does that include . . . any*one*?"

"Not friends, of course! Just everything else. The whole chimichanga."

"You mean 'the whole enchilada'?" Pep said.

"That too," the chupacabra said, finishing off
his eighteenth piece of goat cheese . . . plus
the plate and napkin.

To Rafael,
my favorite funny
little fuzzball
~ M.T.N.

To Ro,
the bravest of all
~ A.A.

NANCY PAULSEN BOOKS
an imprint of Penguin Random House LLC
375 Hudson Street
New York, NY 10014

Manufactured in China by RR Donnelley Asia Printing Solutions Ltd.
ISBN 9780399174438
1 3 5 7 9 10 8 6 4 2

Design by Marikka Tamura. Text set in Fred Bold.
The illustrations were done in watercolor, inks, gouache, and
cochineal with spices and orange on watercolor paper.